Danny –
All the Best!

Jane Cooper

Willie and the Tomato Garden

Jane Helen Cooper

Illustrated by Diane Woods

Hugo House Publishers, Ltd.

Willie and the Tomato Garden.

ISBN: 978-1-936449-77-4

Illustrations: Diane Woods, www.dianewoodsdesign.com

Book Cover Design & Interior Layout: Ronda Taylor, www.rondataylor.com

Hugo House Publishers, Ltd.

Denver, Colorado
Austin, Texas
www.HugoHousePublishers.com

To all my children. . .

Stephanie, Jill, Missy, Tommy
Michael, Yvonne, Danny

and grandchildren . . .

Adam, Ava, Amanda, Annabelle, Caroline,
Cassidy, Cooper, Gregory, Julia, Nick, Oliver, Rachel,
Raymond, Robby, Shannon, Spencer, Wyatte

Willie *loved* tomatoes. She couldn't wait until summer when she could sneak into the garden and eat all the tomatoes she wanted. Even though she would get in big trouble every year, it didn't matter. In the winter, Mr. Oliver, her owner, bought tomatoes for her at the grocery store, but they just didn't smell or taste the same. Maybe it had something to do with that wonderful summer sunshine that felt so deliciously good on her tummy when she turned over to have Mr. Oliver pet her.

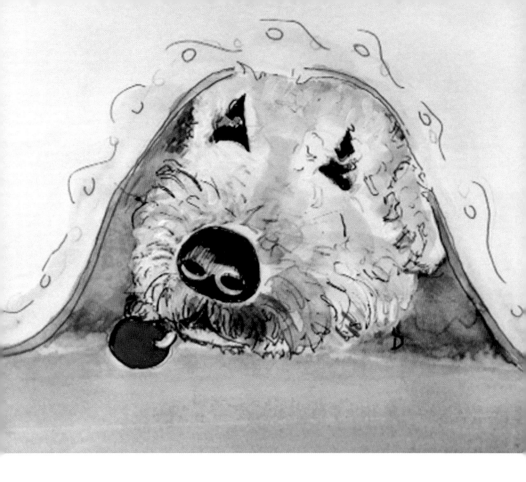

It was just after all the firecrackers had gone off. "Thank goodness that's over!" Willie thought with a sigh of relief. She would hide under the bed, even though the space was too small and really uncomfortable. The *only* thing that made it bearable was that she knew she could go to the garden the next day, and probably—hopefully—find her first ripe, juicy tomato.

The next morning she went hunting. There was no gate on the garden, not even a fence, but that was just fine with Willie. She could start hunting wherever her heart desired. "If only all the tomatoes were red and ripe," sighed Willie as she wandered up and down the long rows, sniffing each plant. Ripe tomatoes growing on the vine had the most wonderful sweet smell, and there was nothing like the taste of a red, juicy tomato in the whole wide world.

It was still early in the summer, so most of the tomatoes were green. Willie sniffed and pushed aside the green plants with her nose, which made her sneeze a lot. The green leaves smelled icky, and there was always something about them that tickled her nose.

Although annoying at times, these things never made her give up. "I can't wait to take a bite of a juicy tomato!" she thought to herself. She took a break to look up through the leaves of the giant oak tree that stood like a statue next to the garden. It was her napping tree, and its branches spread far and out, allowing just enough of the sun's warm rays to shine through its leaves.

Willie loved the feel of the sunshine on her shaggy fur, and how the breeze would rustle the leaves every now and again, just enough to lift her fur and cool her off, keeping her comfortable on a hot summer day.

"I bet that's why these tomatoes taste so good," Willie thought. "They like the sun coming through the trees, just like I do." And that was exactly right. Mr. Oliver knew that for the tomato plants to grow tall and green, they needed just a kiss of sunlight.

"There will be many ripe tomatoes soon enough," Mr. Oliver said to Willie sternly as he stepped into the garden to water each tomato plant with the garden hose. Even though he was unhappy that Willie ate most of his tomatoes every year, he didn't have the heart to stop her yearly rummaging through his garden. He knew how much Willie loved tomatoes. He loved them too. He just wished he could find a way to get Willie to understand how to share them.

Mr. Oliver knew his dog. Even though she obviously couldn't tell him this, Willie not only looked forward to eating tomatoes, she also looked forward to having the tomato garden all to herself.

As Willie walked past the last row of tomato plants, she heard a loud *crunching* noise coming from some tall grass nearby, "What's that?" she asked herself, as her ears stood straight up. She did not want any unwelcome guests coming near her tomatoes.

Upon careful consideration of what was possibly causing the strange noise, Willie concluded, "That *crunching* noise sounds like an eating noise, and it's happening very close to my garden!" Walking a bit closer, she saw a roly-poly groundhog stuffing one dandelion leaf after another into its mouth.

"Munch, munch, munch," chewed the groundhog, unaware that Willie was watching.

"Maybe I can scare this groundhog away if it sees me," Willie thought to herself as she walked even closer, accidently stepping on a twig. The CRACK was so loud, the groundhog looked up, saw Willie, turned around and ran as fast as he could through the tall grass. If dogs could laugh, Willie would have howled as she watched the roly-poly rodent trip and roll over tree roots and rocks, crashing into the big oak tree as he skidded to a sudden stop by his home, a rather large hole in the ground.

The groundhog swiftly jumped into his hole head first, but he got stuck! He had eaten so many dandelions, his tummy was too big to get through the opening. He was now securely wedged half way into his hole, his hind feet sticking straight up in the air, kicking back and forth.

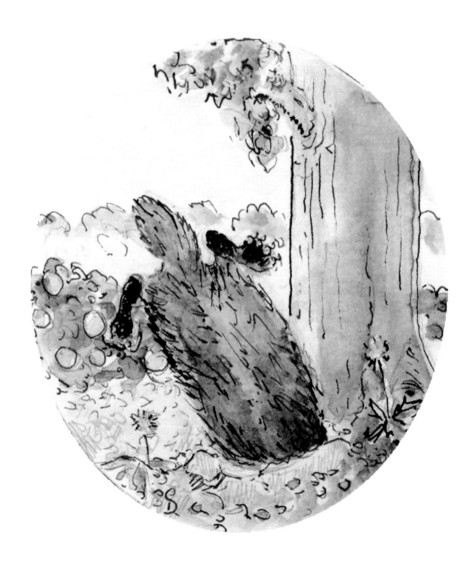

"That dog will surely eat me!" feared the groundhog, even though Willie had no thought of doing any such thing. Willie watched in amazement as the groundhog's body bounced up and down, twisted back and forth, and wiggled itself lower and lower, until finally she heard a loud "*whomp*" and the groundhog's feet disappeared from sight.

"Whew! Sure am glad he's gone!" Willie thought to herself as she walked back into the garden to continue hunting for a ripe tomato. No sooner had she walked past the first plant, when she spotted a green lumpy, bumpy worm taking a large bite out of a green tomato.

"Chomp, chomp, chomp," the plump little creature eagerly took one bite and then another. Willie, now very concerned, was not sure she approved of this intruder eating her tomatoes, even if they were green. She gave the worm a push with her round black nose.

"You know, it's not polite to bother someone while they're eating!" scolded the worm, with cheeks full of green tomato, and irritated that Willie was interrupting her breakfast.

"You happen to be eating one of my tomatoes!" exclaimed Willie, poking her nose even closer.

"… and it's not polite to talk and chew at the same time!" Willie continued, now extremely troubled, realizing that this conversation was getting nowhere.

"Humph!" said the lumpy, bumpy worm turning its back on Willie, deciding to ignore her altogether.

Willie did not know what to do. She had made the groundhog go away, and she had tried to get rid of the worm by pushing it with her nose, but the worm did not budge. It actually didn't care. In fact, in no time at all, it had chewed a very big hole in the tomato!

"What if this worm eats all of the tomatoes, and there are none left for me?" worried Willie.

Just then, "squawk! ... squawk, squawk," yelled a noisy blackbird perching itself on a bird feeder full of sunflower seeds that hung from a branch on the oak tree.

"Now what?" thought Willie, as if encountering a strange-looking worm and a bumbling groundhog hadn't been enough for one morning.

Her curiosity got the better of her. Willie left the worm to finish its breakfast and walked closer to the oak tree. She wanted to get a better look at what was making that awful squawking noise. The large blackbird was happily cracking open one sunflower seed after another with its sharp yellow beak, spitting and scattering seed shells in every direction. As Willie got closer, some even landed on her head and nose, which she did not like at all.

"Hey, watch where you're tossing those things!" Willie shouted to the blackbird, shaking the seed shells off. Impatiently, the blackbird turned its head toward Willie, while spitting more seed shells in her direction. But as the bird turned, it gasped.

"Oh my! Look at all those tomatoes over there. I bet they have plenty of tasty seeds in them!"

"Don't even think about eating the seeds of my tomatoes!" scolded Willie while shaking more seed shells off her nose.

"You wouldn't want a bird to go hungry, would you?" teased the sassy bird, as it turned its back on Willie and continued to peck at more sunflower seeds.

"You can't be hungry … you haven't stopped eating!" exclaimed Willie.

"I'm always hungry!" laughed the bird.

Finally, after cracking the last sunflower seed, the bird flew away. Willie returned to the garden hoping to find at least one juicy ripe tomato before they were all gone.

"You know, you will get a tummy ache if you eat too many of those red tomatoes," Mr. Oliver warned, as he walked up behind Willie in the garden, scratching the shaggy brown fur behind her ears. Willie did not want to hear any such thing.

"Just *one* tomato would certainly not make me sick," she thought, more determined than ever to continue her hunt for ripe tomatoes.

She could almost taste them as she walked up and down every row of tomato plants, sniffing for that yummy tomato smell that she looked forward to each summer. As she stuck her nose deep into the thick leaves, she sensed it—the smell she had been waiting for.

"Wow, that's a big one!" she thought in disbelief, her eyes wide with excitement as she stared at the biggest tomato she had ever seen.

"How am I going to eat it?" she wondered, as she backed her nose away from the thick leaves. And then she had an excellent idea.

Willie pushed and pushed at the tomato with her nose, nudging it this way and that, until she heard it "*plop*" on the ground. Then, holding the tomato firmly between her two front paws, she took one delicious bite and then another until it was all gone. Willie was overjoyed, and she thought with a "humph." Her tummy didn't ache at all.

"Certainly Mr. Oliver must be mistaken," she thought, chuckling to herself. "And because my tummy feels fine, I'm going to eat some more." She found three more tomatoes and then another five, and every time she found a ripe tomato, she ate it, enjoying each one.

In no time at all, Willie lost count of how many tomatoes she had eaten. She was eagerly looking for more when suddenly she stopped right in her tracks. Her tummy didn't feel well at all, and she had to lie down." Perhaps Mr. Oliver was right," she sadly admitted with a groan.

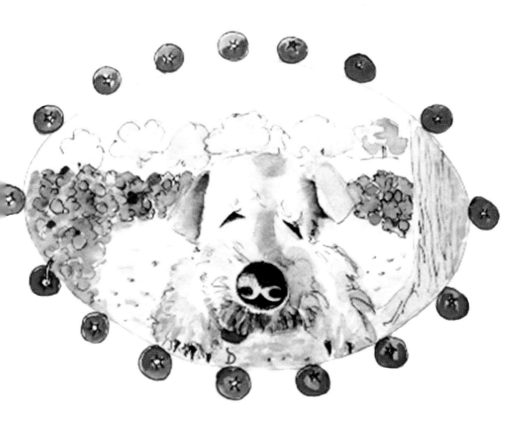

Behind the big oak tree, the roly-poly groundhog curiously peaked out of its hole, sniffing the air.

"What were you eating?" the groundhog asked, continuing to sniff while slowly coming closer to Willie.

"I think I just ate my fifteenth tomato," groaned Willie, looking at the last lonely tomato dangling from a vine.

"Oh my … you look awful," muttered the groundhog, moving closer to Willie while continuing to sniff the air.

"Those tomato leaves sure do smell good! Is it time for lunch yet?"

Willie laid her head between her paws and closed her eyes. Just the thought of the smell of tomato leaves made her feel worse.

"Eat as many as you want," she moaned, wanting to be left alone in her misery.

"Oh that's wonderful!" cheered the happy groundhog, as he shuffled over to a leafy tomato plant and began munching on the leaves.

All that commotion made the lumpy, bumpy

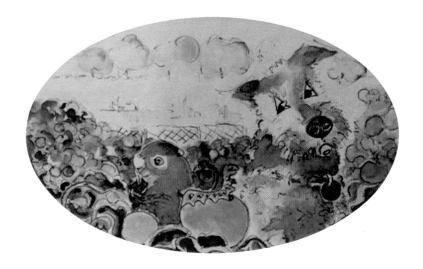

tomato worm look up from eating her lunch on yet another green tomato. She inched over to get a closer look at Willie.

"What have you done?" the worm asked in a tiny worried voice.

Willie opened one eye and moaned again, "oooohhh." But just as she was going to answer the worm, she let out a loud *"BUUUUURRRP!"* instead.

"You really got carried away, didn't you?" asked the worm, while looking sternly at Willie.

"I didn't eat any *green* tomatoes, so there are plenty *(burp)* over there. Help *(burp)* yourself *(burp)*," said Willie as she struggled to stop burping, pointing her nose in the direction of a tall plant full of green tomatoes.

"Good to know you can share when you want to!" replied the worm, as it happily inched up to the top of the tomato plant and found a large green tomato to munch on.

The noisy blackbird, perched on a branch of the big oak tree, had been listening to Willie's conversation with the worm and the groundhog.

"Looks like I'm not the only one with a big appetite! Sorry you're a little sick, but is there anything left?" eagerly asked the blackbird, as it flew down closer to Willie, looking to see if there were any leftover seeds on the ground.

"There's one tomato over there," sighed Willie, looking back at the single, lonely tomato dangling on the vine. So the hungry blackbird eagerly hopped over to where the fruit hung low to the ground, and pecked at it with its sharp, yellow beak until it reached the moist seeds inside. The bird ate and ate, not stopping until it had eaten every seed.

Willie had never felt as sick as she did that day, and realized that she should have listened to Mr. Oliver's warning. She also realized she was being selfish in keeping the tomato garden all to herself.

"Maybe I should allow that strange little worm to have a green tomato for breakfast now and then. I don't even like green tomatoes. That goofy groundhog is really quite nice and enjoys eating the tomato leaves. The blackbird is always hungry, and there are plenty of seeds in just one tomato. Sharing the garden would make everybody happy," she reasoned, a smile now appearing on her furry face. She felt all warm and happy from the top of her ears to the tip of her tail.

Willie yawned and decided that she had enough excitement for one day. Besides, a nap might make her tummy ache go away. Finding a soft place in the middle of the tomato garden, she fell asleep and dreamed of walking up and down the rows of tomato plants just as she had done that day, but in her dream she looked for more tomatoes to share with her new friends.

Starting that day, something wonderful happened. Willie shared her tomato garden with the roly-poly groundhog, the lumpy bumpy worm, and the noisy blackbird.

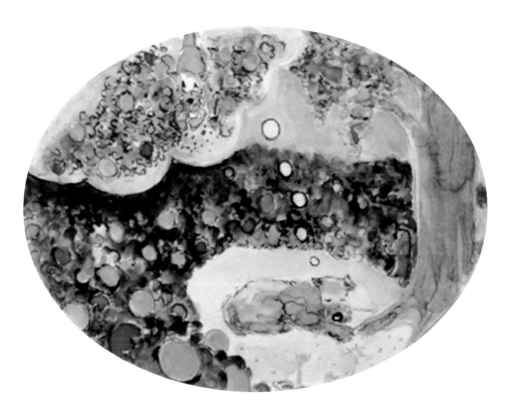

Mr. Oliver was happy because Willie had something else to do which kept her out of trouble. Willie was happy because she made three new friends who were always willing to have a feast with her whenever they all wanted. And her three new friends were happy because they always knew they could find a friendly meal in the tomato garden.

Even though Willie loved tomatoes, she learned that eating too many will make her sick, just as Mr. Oliver had warned. But she also learned that gardens are for sharing, and sharing with others is a very good way to make new friends.

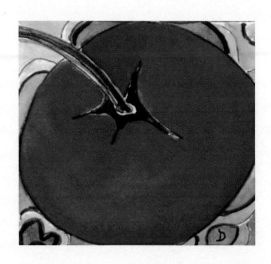

Acknowledgements

To my husband, Larry, who tolerated my reading this story aloud to him more than just a few times, and who encouraged me and supported me for the last five years as I persevered in writing this story.

To my children, Stephanie, Jill, Missy, and Tommy who spurred me on to finish this book. A special thanks to Jill and husband, Jim, for nurturing Willie for the first seven years of her life, and then entrusting us with her for five remaining never-a-dull moment years.

To Hugo House Publishing/Banyan Tree Press, especially my editor, Patricia Ross, for sharing her expertise, wisdom, humor, and guidance to this story, helping to make it the best it can be—and for really good phone conversations, which I will miss.

To my illustrator, Diane Woods, whose illustrations immediately touched my heart through her capturing the essence of Willie, and bringing three little characters to life through the creation of her beautiful artwork.

And finally, to my mother, Wilda, for inspiring me to write through sharing her love of the written word, along with her encouragement and example.

About the Author

This is Jane Helen Cooper's first children's book. Jane and her husband, Larry, have a blended family of seven children and seventeen grandchildren. They are both retired and live in North Royalton, Ohio. After Jane left her thirty-year career in administration and customer service, she decided to finish her undergraduate degree. Graduating with honors, she received her Bachelor's degree in 2014, from Baldwin Wallace University, majoring in English and Creative Writing. Jane's other works include the publication of some of her poetry in the Baldwin Wallace literary magazine, *The Mill*. Jane and her husband like to travel, enjoy home remodeling, and spending time with their children and grandchildren.

About the Illustrator

Illustrator, Diane Woods, fell in love at the first sight of Willie in a photograph sent to her by author, Jane Helen Cooper. She and Jane have delighted in the entire process of bringing Willie and the Tomato Garden to life. May you share their delight in this story of an adorable dog who learns a valuable lesson about sharing.

Diane was born in Winona, MN, raised in San Francisco, graduated high school in Poitiers, France, and has adored living in the wine country north of San Francisco where her daughter, Kenna, lives. She now loves living and painting in Austin, TX. Her work may be viewed at: https://dianewoodsdesign.com/